THE SESAME STREET STORYBOOK

Stories and Verse Based on Material
from the Sesame Street Show

featuring

JIM HENSON'S MUPPETS

verse adaptations by

ALBERT G. MILLER

illustrated by

KELLY OECHSLI, MEL CRAWFORD
MARY LOU DETTMER, MIKE FRITH

Published by Random House in conjunction with the Children's Television Workshop.

CONTENTS

SESAME STREET

Executive Producer: David D. Connell
Producer: Jon Stone
Head Writer: Jeffrey Moss
Writers: Jerry Juhl, Emily Kaplin,
Bob Oksner, Ray Sipherd, Norman Stiles,
Jon Stone, Dan Wilcox

This title was originally catalogued by the Library of Congress as follows: The Sesame Street storybook; stories and verse based on material from the Sesame Street show, featuring Jim Henson's muppets. Verse adaptations by Albert G. Miller. Illustrated by Kelly Oechsli [and others. New York] Random House [c1971] 63 p. col. illus. 29 cm. $3.95. SUMMARY: Stories and verse featuring characters from the television show introduce number concepts, letters of the alphabet, and word meanings. 1. Children's literature (Collections) [1. Literature—Collections] I. Miller, Albert G., 1905– II. Oechsli, Kelly, illus. III. Sesame Street. PZ5.S48 810'.8'09282 70–158385 ISBN 0-394-82332-X : 0-394-92332-4 (lib. bdg.)

ERNIE
PRESENTS
THE LETTER A

Now it's time to study the letter **A**. One word that begins with **A** is **APPLE**.

This is an **APPLE**. Do you know what to do with an **APPLE**?

You eat it. Ha-ha.

THE PRINCESS
AND THE COOKIE

In a castle on a mountain
There was once a friendly King,
And he would have been quite happy
But for one annoying thing;
What upset him was a problem
That disturbed him night and day:
It was how to find a husband
For his daughter Princess Kay.

"I am tiny," said the Princess,
"Very delicate and sweet.
I will marry any fellow
Who can bake my best-loved treat.
Do you know what that is, Daddy?
Do you know my favorite thing?
Do you know what I'm so hooked on?"
"Sure, it's COOKIES!" said the King.

"Yes, my greatest treat is COOKIES,"
Said the Princess with a sigh,
"But they must be small and dainty,
And as delicate as I.
If a man who baked such cookies
Came to visit me," said Kay,
"I would fall in love that *minute.*
I would marry him that day!"

Said the King, "A dozen princes
Have brought cookies here to taste.
But the trouble that they went to—
It was just a total waste!
When you taste their sample cookies
You've but one rude word to say.
Can you tell me what the word is?"
"Sure, it's 'BLECCH'," said Princess Kay.

5

"That is right," her dad continued,
"And it pains my royal neck
When you nibble on a cookie,
Hold your nose, and holler 'BLECCH!'
You are mighty picky, daughter!
I can *not* believe it's true
That those princes' homemade cookies
Were not good enough for you."

"Bring a fellow," said the Princess,
"With a cookie in his paw
That is tiny and delicious,
And you'll have a son-in-law."
Said her dad, "Three handsome princes
Have arrived from distant lands.
They are waiting in the parlor,
Holding cookies in their hands."

In the castle's royal parlor
Stood a prince in uniform.
"Here's a cookie, dear," he whispered,
"Better eat it while it's warm."
Said the King, "Boy, that's so tiny,
It's no bigger than a speck.
What's the word for this one, daughter?"
Said the royal Princess: "BLECCH!"

Then the prince said, "You're bananas!"
Stamped his foot upon the floor,
Threw the cookie on the table
And went marching out the door.
"*He's* bananas," said the Princess,
"That one will not do at all!
That cookie is not *tiny* . . .
I would say it's only . . . small!"

SMALL

When the second prince was summoned,
In he pranced in shining armor.
"Take this cookie, babe," he murmured,
"I just baked it—it's a charmer."

"That's just *your* opinion, Charlie,"
Said the Princess with a pout.
"Leave your cookie on the table
And my maid will show you out."

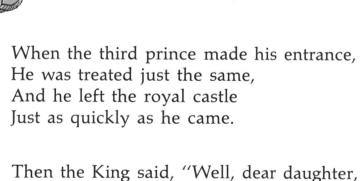

When the third prince made his entrance,
He was treated just the same,
And he left the royal castle
Just as quickly as he came.

Then the King said, "Well, dear daughter,
You have made your dad a wreck.
You will never find a husband
'Cause you're always saying 'BLECCH!'"

8

Just about a minute later,
From the castle kitchen wing,
There appeared the Cookie Monster,
Private baker to the King.
In his hand the baker carried,
On a teeny-weeny tray,
One delicious-looking cookie—
Small and delicate as Kay.

"Made this cookie," said the Monster,
"Smallest one you'll ever meet.
Well, so long, old King and Princess,
Gonna take outside and eat."
"*Hold that cookie!*" cried the Princess,
"It's the one I long for. WOW!
Let me eat your perfect cookie
And I'll marry you right now."

"Nothin' doin'!" said the Monster,
"Cookie made for me alone!"
"But," the King said, "give it to her
And you'll sit upon a throne!
Give that cookie to my daughter
And who knows how far you'll go.
You'll no longer be a baker,
But a *prince* with lots of dough."

"No! No! No!" exclaimed the Monster.
But then, looking down, he saw
Three more cookies that were lying
On the table near his paw.
"Cookies!" bellowed Cookie Monster,
"Great *big* cookies! Son-of-gun!"
Cried the King, "Then trade them! Trade them!
Give my Kay your tiny one!"

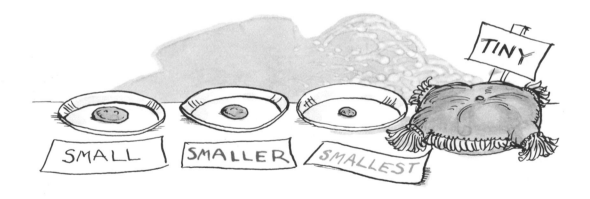

"Oh boy!" said the Cookie Monster,
"It's a deal—I eat these three!
Princess Kay can eat *my* cookie,
But no have to marry me."
"But you MUST!" the King commanded,
Hugging him around the neck,
"Welcome to the family, baker."
Said the Cookie Monster: "BLECCH!"

ERNIE PRESENTS
THE LETTER
Q

THE BOY, THE GIRL AND THE JELLYBEANS

CHAPTER ONE

One day a boy was skipping merrily down the street, talking happily to himself.

"Boy, am I happy!" he whooped. "I've got a bag stuffed with jellybeans! And I'm crazy about jellybeans! I *love* jellybeans!"

Suddenly, the boy heard a girl crying. "Hey, girl," the boy said, "how come you're crying?"

"I'm crying because I'm sad," the girl moaned. "I'm *really* unhappy."

"That's strange," said the boy. "I'm feeling great! What's wrong?"

The girl wiped away a knuckleful of tears. "I lost my jellybeans," she sobbed. "That's what's wrong. And jellybeans are just wonderful. Did you ever lose *your* jellybeans?"

"Lose my jellybeans!" yelled the boy. "You must be bananas!"

"Then you can't know how I feel," she wept. "You would have to lose *your* jellybeans to know how sad I am."

"Wait a second," said the boy.
"I've got a whole bag full of
jellybeans here."

"You have?" said the girl.

"I sure have! And do you know
what? I'm feeling *so* happy and *so*
good, maybe I'll give them to you."

"You will?" she yelled. "Oh joy!"

"Yes, yes, I will! I will! Here, take
them! Take them! Take the whole bag!"

The girl grabbed the bag. "Hey," she shrieked happily. "This is fantastic! I've got jellybeans! I feel great! Wonderful! HAPPY! Thanks a lot, boy." And clutching the bag of jellybeans, she ran off down the street.

"Wow!" the boy said, really pleased with himself. "I sure am pleased with myself. I really cheered her up by giving her my jellybeans. Hey, wait just a minute!" he cried. "I loved my jellybeans. I adored my jellybeans! But I gave my jellybeans away! *Oh no!* How could I do it?"

The boy burst into tears. "Oh, am I SAD!" he bawled. "Oh, am I UNHAPPY!" he sobbed. "Other people could never know how sad I am. Unless," he sniffled, "they'd lost *their* jellybeans, too . . ."

TO BE CONTINUED . . .

OSCAR CHOOSES A PET

"I've been thinking," Oscar muttered,
"Of the pleasant life I lead,
Living in this filthy trashcan—
It is very nice indeed!

But it might be even better
If I had a little pet,
Though it's kind of hard to figure
Just what animal to get."

"I could never think of puppies,
'Cause they wag their tails all day,
And they're lovable and darling,
So I'd hate them right away.

Tiny kittens are no better,
For they're cute, beyond a doubt,
And they're always washing whiskers,
So the kittens, man, are out."

Oscar thought another minute,
Then he almost flipped his wig.
"Holy smoke!" he cried, "I've got it!
I will buy myself a *pig!*

Since a pig is fat and filthy,
I would love him like a cousin.
What a roommate for my trashcan!
Hey! I think I'll buy a *dozen!*"

ERNIE DUSTS THE SHELF

One morning when Bert returned home from the store,
He found Ernie mumbling and walking the floor.
"What's wrong with you, Ernie, old buddy?" he said,
"How come you are talking and scratching your head?"

"There's something," said Ernie, "that I have forgotten.
Forgetting it makes me feel stupid and rotten.
It's something that I've got to do for myself
Before I start dusting this toy-covered shelf."

"This toy shelf," Bert snorted, "needs plenty of dusting.
The way you are stalling is simply disgusting!
Just look at the dirt on your poor rubber duckie.
He's dusty, he's grimy, he's filthy, he's *yucchy!*"

"I'm really not stalling," said Ernie. "It's *true*
That I can't remember the thing I must do
Before the dust-up of the shelf has begun.
I *know* it's important. It *has* to be done."

"Get busy, you meatball!" Bert shouted. "You *must!*
Quit stalling! Start working! Get rid of that dust!"
"Okay," Ernie said, "if you say so, I'll do it.
I'll skip what I had to do first and get to it!"

He rushed to the shelf, and with one mighty sweep
He whisked all the toys to the floor in a heap,
And though some were bent and broken and shattered,
The shelf was now clean and that's all that mattered.

Poor Bert pointed down to the toys at their feet.
"You birdbrain!" he hollered. "Good gosh! Holy Pete!
You're cuckoo! Bananas! Your brain must be busting!
Why didn't you take the toys *off* before dusting?"

"That's *it!*" shouted Ernie, just jumping for joy.
"Hey, thanks for reminding me, old buddy boy.
You take the toys *off* before dusting the shelf!
That's what I was trying to think of my*self!*"

As Bert knocked his head on the edge of the bed,
Ernie picked up his dear duckie and said,
"I'm happy that I was reminded by Bert,
But happier still that my duckie's not hurt."

20

THE BOY, THE GIRL AND THE JELLYBEANS

CHAPTER TWO

One afternoon a boy was walking down the street. Just that morning he had given away his only bag of jellybeans, and that had made him feel very sad. But now he was beginning to get over it.

"Well, I don't have any jellybeans," he said to himself, "but that's okay. I can do without jellybeans. I'm a cool customer who doesn't need any jellybeans to get along in this world. I'm cool and I'm confident, brother, and nothing, NOTHING, can bother me."

He turned a corner and there he saw a girl. It was the very same girl he had given his bag of jellybeans to. And she still had it. She was clutching the bag in her hands and shaking like a thistle in a windstorm.

"Hey, girl," said the boy, "what's the matter with you?"

"I'm afraid!" said the girl. "I'm really, really scared. I'm so frightened that I've got goose bumps on my goose bumps."

"Huh!" said the boy. "I'm never afraid. I'm cool and I'm confident and nothing, NOTHING, bothers me. What's your problem?"

"*Problem?*" The girl's eyes grew wide. "A MONSTER is my problem. A great BIG monster has been after me."

"Pish-tosh," said the boy, "that's nothing to be afraid of. It certainly wouldn't frighten *me*."

"Oh yeah?" said the girl. "Did you ever have a monster after *you?*"

"Well . . . no," said the boy.

"There!" said the girl, still trembling with fear. "Then you don't know how scary it is. It's really frightening to have a great big UGLY monster after you."

"Phoo," said the boy. "I wouldn't be afraid. If he shows up again, I'll frighten *him* away."

"Really?" said the girl. "That's very nice of you. That's so nice, I'm going to give you back your jellybeans. Here, take them." She handed him the jellybeans and stopped trembling right away.

"I feel better now," she said. "I feel confident. I don't have a worry in the world."

"That's right," said the boy, "because there's nothing to worry about. Just be like me—I'm *never* afraid. *Yikes!*"

The boy screamed, for just then a great big ugly HAIRY monster came around the corner and headed straight for him.

"Oh me," moaned the boy. "Oh my, oh my. I'm so frightened. I'm so afraid that I'm afraid . . . I mean, I'm so scared that I'm scared . . . I mean, I'm so afraid that I'm trembling. Ohhhh."

"Really?" said the girl. "Well, I'm not at all afraid. Not a bit. Do you want to know why?"

"Why?" asked the shaking boy.

"Because," the girl answered, "that monster loves jellybeans. He was only after me because I had the jellybeans. But now *you* have the jellybeans. So he is not after ME any more. He is after

YOU. So you see, now I don't have anything to be afraid of." And, waving good-by, she skipped off down the street.

"JELLYBEANS!" roared the great big ugly hairy blue monster. "ME SMELL JELLYBEANS!"

"H-here, pal," squeaked the boy. "Have mine." And he quickly poured them all into the monster's great big ugly hairy blue paw.

"YUM! YUM!" roared the monster, swallowing them all in a gulp. "DELICIOUS! THANK YOU!" And he gave the boy a big wet hairy blue kiss right on the top of the head.

Then, arm in arm, the boy and the monster walked off down the street like a couple of old friends. And the boy wasn't frightened any more.

TO BE CONTINUED . . .

 # BERT  PRESENTS THE NUMBER 5

24

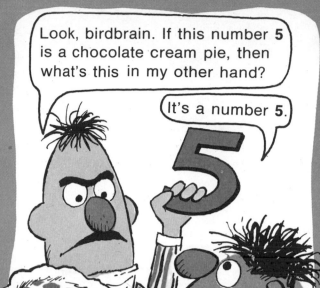

SHAPES OF THINGS TO EAT

Listen, children, while I sing about
How I'm gonna eat
Three different **SHAPES** of things for lunch,
Here on Sesame Street.

Gonna start right in with a birdseed sandwich
Made on tasty rye . . .
Then top it off with a birdseed cookie
And a piece of birdseed pie!

Shape of the sandwich
Is a **SQUARE** . . .

Cookie
Is a **CIRCLE** neat . . .

Piece of pie
Is a **TRIANGLE** . . .
What a shapely treat!

Three different shapes
Of things to eat . . .

Here . . . on . . .

Sesame Street.

THE BOY, THE GIRL AND THE JELLYBEANS

CHAPTER THREE

Early one evening, a boy who was crazy about jellybeans was walking down the street feeling very angry. That morning he had given his jellybeans to a girl he'd met. And that afternoon he had just gotten the jellybeans back when a monster came along and ate them all up. So the boy had lost his jellybeans twice in one day, and just thinking about it made him very, very mad.

"Boy, am I mad," he said to himself as he walked along. "If you lose your jellybeans once it makes you sad. But if you lose them twice it makes you *mad*. Now all I have left is my empty jellybean bag. No *wonder* I'm mad."

Just then he turned the corner, and there he saw the girl he had given his jellybeans to that morning. In front of her was a table with a pile of jellybeans on it and she was talking angrily to herself.

"Boy, am I mad," the girl said. "I'm so angry I could *scream*. I think I *will* scream." And she did and the boy heard her, because it was so loud.

"Hey," said the boy. "Why are you screaming like that?"

"Because I'm *mad*," she grumped. "I'm in a rotten mood."

"Me, too," scowled the boy. "And I bet I'm madder than you are."

"Ha!" she snorted. "That's what you think. You don't know what mad *is* until you're as mad as I am."

"Yeah? What're you so mad about?"

"I found these jellybeans. I thought I'd lost them, but I found them right here on the table."

The boy frowned. "That's why you're mad? That's nothing to be *mad* about."

"I'm not mad about *finding* these jellybeans," she shouted. "I'm mad because *I don't have anything to put them in!* So I can't take them home."

"Why not eat them here?" the boy suggested.

"How can I? It's almost dinnertime. If I eat these jellybeans now, they'll spoil my dinner. So I'll just have to stay here forever and ever looking at them, because I don't have anything to put them in and *that's* why I'm mad."

"Phooey," said the boy, "that's nothing. Let me tell you what *I'm* mad about. I lost my jellybeans twice today—once to you and once to a monster. And I'll never get them back because the monster ate them, and so all I have is an empty jellybean bag and that's why I'm mad."

"Well," said the girl, "that's nothing to be mad ab–" She stopped and looked at the boy. "You have an *empty* jellybean bag?"

"Sure, but what difference does–?" The boy pointed at the table. "*You* have jellybeans?"

"Yes, I have," she said sweetly.

He smiled. "What do you know? I have a bag to put them in."

"Hey," she said, "I'm not mad anymore."

"Neither am I."

The girl laughed. "Hey, want to come to my house for dinner?"

"Sure," said the boy, "but–uh– what're we going to have?"

"Jellybeans, of course. Okay?"

"O-*kay!* Here . . . pour your jellybeans into my bag," said the boy. And she did.

And so there were jellybeans for everybody! Isn't that a good way to end the story?

THE END!

In this story there are dozens of words that begin with the letter D. So listen carefully and see how many D-words you can count. This story is called

THE DIAMOND D
AND THE DREADFUL DRAGON

ozens of years ago, in a drafty castle, Duke David of Dundeedle did dwell. Duke David was dumpy, but dignified. And he had a darling daughter named Dora who was a delight.

One day Dora danced through the door in a dear little dress decorated with daffodils. "Doodley-doo, doodley-doo," Dora sang, as she danced. "Oh, hello, dear, dumpy daddy," said Dora to Duke David of Dundeedle.

"Dora, my darling, dimpled daughter," said Duke David. "You are indeed delightful, so I have a dandy present for you."

"Do tell," said Dora. "Do describe this doo-dad, daddy."

"It is a dazzling diamond D dangling from a chain!" So, hanging the D around Dora's dimpled neck, Duke David of Dundeedle departed through the door.

Dora also departed, darting down into the daisy patch to dance amid the Duke's downy ducks.

Although Dora and Duke David didn't know it, someone else dwelt in the castle. This someone was Donald, the Dreadful Dragon of Dundeedle.

"I am Donald, the Dreadful Dragon of Dundeedle. I live in a dungeon downstairs in Duke David's dwelling. It is a deep dungeon, a dark dungeon—a deep, dark, damp, dank, dreary dungeon. It is a dump!"

Donald used dozens of D words—which was the only nice thing you could say about him. Otherwise he was a dud.

Donald the Dragon dashed from his dungeon, directly to Duke David's dandy daisy patch. "I am dashing from my dungeon to steal the diamond D that Duke David gave his daughter Dora," he said.

Donald, the doer of dark deeds, drifted into the daisy patch. Dora, daughter of Duke David, saw the dreadful dragon and dropped a drooping daisy from her dainty dimpled hand. She danced directly up to Donald the Dragon and declared, "Well, look who's here—a dear doggie! Hi there, doggie."

Donald disbelieved his droopy ears. "*Doggie?*" he screamed. "Did you say *doggie?*"

"Definitely," said Dora.

"Well, I do declare!" said Donald. "If Dora, the dignified Duke David's daughter, thinks that I, Donald the Dreadful Dragon of Dundeedle, am a doggie, then Dora is *dumb!*"

"But you're the dearest doggie I've ever seen," Dora declared. "Do come and dwell in our castle, doggie dear, and I'll give you this Diamond D which my doting daddy draped around my dimpled neck."

"Don't 'doggie' me!" Donald roared, darting toward Dora, determined to grab the Diamond D.

Suddenly, Duke David dashed into the daisy patch. Diving between darling Dora and Dreadful Donald, the Duke drove Donald around and around the daisy patch. The dismal dragon ducked, dodged, darted and dashed through the ducklings and the daisies until the Duke dumped him into the duck pond.

"Daddy dear," said Dora, "why did you do that?"

"Because that dreadful, dishonest dragon was determined to steal the dazzling Diamond D from around your dainty, dimpled neck," said the Duke.

"Dragon?" said Dora. "I'll be darned! He looked like a doggie to *me.*"

"You're dumb but you're adorable, Dora," said Duke David, "so here's what we'll do. From this day on this dreadful dragon will dwell in a dog house, dine on dog biscuits, and do doggie tricks to delight my divine daughter Dora—*or else!*"

"Or else what?" Donald demanded.

"I'll dump you in the duck pond again!"

"Bow-wow," said Donald. "I'm a doggie."

And so David, Duke of Dundeedle, and his delightful daughter Dora lived happily ever after with Donald the Doggie who used to be a dreadful dragon.

37

ERNIE PRESENTS THE LETTER U

Now let's study the letter **U**. The word **UKULELE** begins with the letter **U**. Do you know what to do with a **UKULELE**?

Oh, no! Not again!

He eats anything! Now he's going to eat my ukulele.

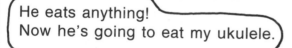

Lookie, lookie, lookie— here comes cookie!

Hello, everybodee! This is your old friend, Grover, flying up in the sky in my little pink airplane.

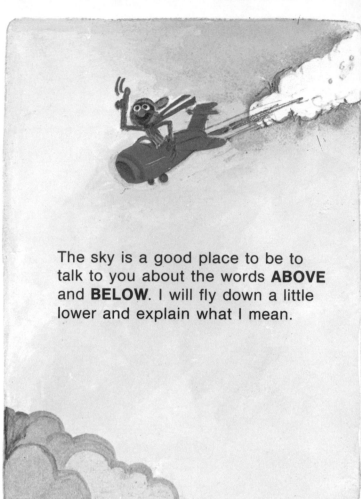

The sky is a good place to be to talk to you about the words **ABOVE** and **BELOW**. I will fly down a little lower and explain what I mean.

See those trees down there? I, Grover, am **ABOVE** the trees. The trees are **BELOW** me.

Now I will fly higher and then I will talk to you some more.

I am much higher now! I am up close to the fluffy white clouds. This cloud is **ABOVE** me. The ground is down **BELOW** me.

Now look out! Up I go, even *higher!*

Here I am—furry, lovable old Grover—flying closer to the hot, yellow sun. The sun is **ABOVE** me. And I am **BELOW** the sun.

Now I am going to fly higher *still!*

I am **ABOVE** you. You are so far **BELOW** me you cannot even see me.

Okay now, fasten your seat belts! We are going down for a landing.

The ground is **BELOW** me, and that is where I am going to land. OOPS! I, Grover, am flying too *fast* in my little airplane.

Next time, I do not think that I, Grover, will talk to you about **ABOVE** and **BELOW**. Next time, I will talk about the lovely word **ON** . . . like **ON** the ground. After this, that is where I think I am going to stay.

ERNIE'S SIX DELICIOUS COOKIES

When peeking through the oven door,
Old Ernie rubbed his tummy.
He had six cookies baking there,
And, boy, did they look yummy!

When they were done he took them out
And put them on a plate.
But finding them too hot to eat,
He settled down to wait.

The moment Ernie took a chair
To watch the cookies cooling,
The Cookie Monster galloped in,
And, brother, was he drooling!

"Cookie! Cookie! Gimme one!"
The Monster cried. "I eat it!"

"Get going, Monster," Ernie said,
"They're all for me, so beat it!"

"Aw, shucks!" the Cookie Monster growled,
And shuffled out the door.
"He gave up easy," Ernie thought.
"He's not done *that* before."

"And now that I'm alone," he said,
"A cookie I will bite."
But then there entered through the door
A stranger dressed in white.

"Me cookie baker," said the man,
"Me taste your cookies, no?"
"Of course," said Ernie, "help yourself.
Take *two* before you go."

The baker wolfed the cookies down
And hurried out the door.

"He loved my cookies," Ernie said,
"But now I've only four."

The moment he sat down again,
Another stranger came:
A little girl with yellow hair,
Who called out Ernie's name.

"Me hungry, Ernie," growled the girl.
"You cookies got for me?"

"I've only four left," Ernie said,
"But I will give you three."

She swallowed all three cookies whole

And galloped out the door.

And Ernie had one cookie left,
Of all his yummy four.

Then Bert came in and said, "Hey, Ern,
I just saw something wild—
The Cookie Monster just came out,
Dressed like a little child."

"The Cookie Monster?" Ernie cried.
"That really makes me sore!
He ate two cookies first time here,
And then he ate three more!"

Said Bert, "I see you saved *me* one,
I'll eat it now, right here."
And snatching Ernie's cookie up,
He made it disappear.

Poor Ernie eyed the empty plate
And groaned, "What happened, son?
You baked six cookies for yourself,
And ate not even one!"

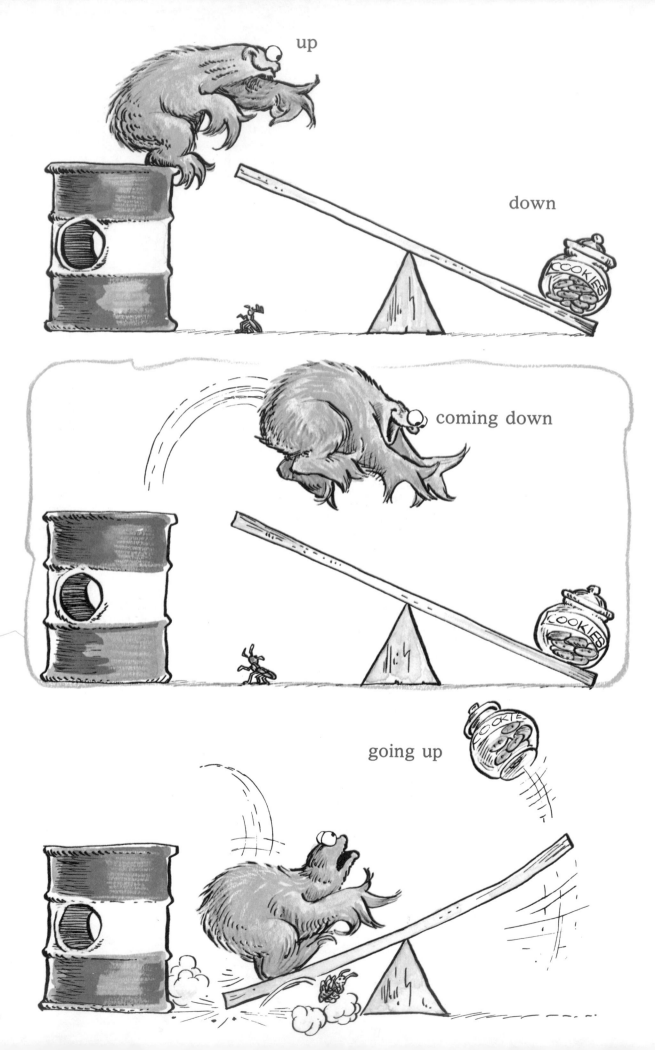

up

down

coming down

going up

50

51

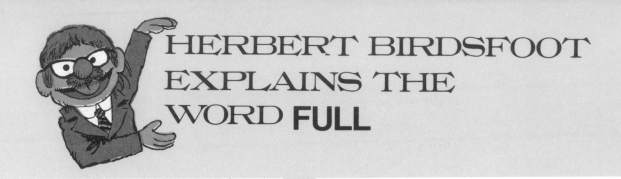

HERBERT BIRDSFOOT EXPLAINS THE WORD FULL

Hi, there. This is your friend, Herbert Birdsfoot. I'm here to tell you about the word **FULL**.

As you can see, this glass is **FULL**. It's **FULL** of yummy strawberry.

Strawberry soda?

Hey, *don't.*

52

THE MAGIC APPLE

There was once a simple farm boy,
Poor but honest as the dickens,
And he worked from dawn to midnight,
Pitching hay and feeding chickens.
"I am poor and I am honest,"
Said the farm boy, "but it's rough
Working every day till midnight
Pitching hay and other stuff."

Thought the poor but honest farm boy,
As he leaned upon his rake,
"If I had one wish to wish for,
There is only one I'd make.
I would wish to trade this barnyard
And this yucchy farm-boy life,
For a dandy golden palace
And a princess for a wife."

He was sound asleep one morning
Underneath an apple tree,
When he heard a great explosion
That was loud as it could be.
BOOM! A lady stood beside him,
Saying, "Hello there, young fella.
I'm your handy fairy god-ma,
Like the one in Cinderella."

55

"Pleased to meet you," said her godson,
As he grinned from ear to ear.
"You're a mighty pretty lady
And I'm glad to see you here."
"Sonny," said the pretty lady,
"I've a big surprise for you:
If there's anything you wish for,
I will see that it comes true."

"Hey, that's groovy!" said the farm boy,
"Golly, I can hardly wait!"
"*One* wish only," said the fairy,
"So you'd better make it great."
Said the boy, "*Two* things I wish for,
Either one and I'd be lucky:
One's a nice banana milkshake . . .
One's a brand new rubber duckie."

"Wait a minute! Are you crazy?
Have you changed your mind?" she cried.
"What you wanted was a palace
And a princess for a bride."
"You're so right, ma'am," said her godson,
"But I think that I'd be lucky
If the palace had a princess,
AND a milkshake, AND a duckie."

"It's a deal," the fairy answered,
Pointing upward in the tree.
"If you pick that magic apple,
What you wish will come to be."
Then there came a loud explosion,
And before her godson spoke,
She had vanished very quickly
In a cloud of purple smoke.

"I can't reach that magic apple,"
Said the farm boy. "Not at all."
So he grabbed the tree and shook it,
But the apple wouldn't fall.

Then he got so tired from shaking
That he tumbled in a heap
Underneath the magic apple,
Where he promptly fell asleep.

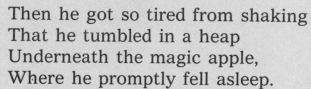

Then his snoring shook the tree trunk
From the bottom to the top,
And the rosy magic apple
Fell into his mouth—KER-PLOP!

"Glugga-mugga," said the farm boy,
"Argha-bargha, google-gapple."
But you couldn't understand him
'Cause his mouth was full of apple.

For awhile he lay there gurgling,
Making lots of silly talk,
Then a wealthy king came strolling
On his daily royal walk.
"Say there, poor but honest farm boy,"
Said the king, "I beg your pardon,
But is that a *magic* apple?"
Said the boy, "Blub-garfer-gardon."

Said his majesty, "I'm sorry,
But I do not understand."
So the boy took out the apple
And he held it in his hand.
"Sure, this apple's *full* of magic,"
Said the boy. "It's *got* to be,
'Cause my fairy god-ma said so,
Underneath this very tree."

"I've been looking for a farm boy
(Poor but honest) since the spring,
Who possessed a magic apple,"
Said the very happy king.
"Will you move into my palace
And be married to my daughter?
You will have your own apartment
With a stove and running water."

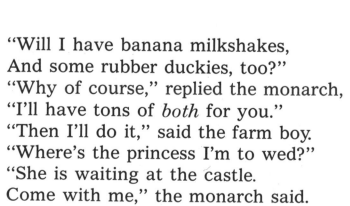

"Will I have banana milkshakes,
And some rubber duckies, too?"
"Why of course," replied the monarch,
"I'll have tons of *both* for you."
"Then I'll do it," said the farm boy.
"Where's the princess I'm to wed?"
"She is waiting at the castle.
Come with me," the monarch said.

When the farm boy saw the princess,
Everybody heard his screams,
For she didn't look exactly
Like the princess of his dreams.
But with duckies and with milkshakes
He lived all his life in clover.
Isn't that a lovely story?
Are you sorry that it's over?

This is your old friend Grover here explaining two words **FAR** . . . . . and **NEAR**.

So here I go like a racing car . . .

I stand way off— we call this **FAR**!

I run right back like a speeding deer . . .

Now I am close. We call this **NEAR**!

I zoom once more like a shooting star . . .

. . . and from where you sit I am quite **FAR**!

When I run back from there to here . . .

. . . and stand beside you I am **NEAR**!

Again I leave you where you are and run like mad till I am . . .

FAR!

I gallop back till I am . . .

NEAR!

62